BILLY BUTTON

Titles in Teen Reads:

BILLY BUTTON
CAVAN SCOTT

DAWN OF THE DAVES
TIM COLLINS

DEAD SCARED
TOMMY DONBAVAND

DEADLY MISSION
MARK WRIGHT

FAIR GAME
ALAN DURANT

JIGSAW LADY
TONY LEE

HOME
TOMMY DONBAVAND

KIDNAP
TOMMY DONBAVAND

MAMA BARKFINGERS
CAVAN SCOTT

PEST CONTROL
CAVAN SCOTT

SITTING TARGET
JOHN TOWNSEND

STALKER
TONY LEE

THE HUNTED
CAVAN SCOTT

THE CORRIDOR
MARK WRIGHT

TROLL
TIM COLLINS

UNDERWORLD
SIMON CHESHIRE

WARD 13
TOMMY DONBAVAND

WORLD WITHOUT WORDS
JONNY ZUCKER

Badger Publishing Limited, Oldmedow Road, Hardwick Industrial Estate, King's Lynn PE30 4JJ
Telephone: 01438 791037

www.badgerlearning.co.uk

BILLY BUTTON

CAVAN SCOTT

Billy Button ISBN 978-1-78147-795-3

Text © Cavan Scott 2014
Complete work © Badger Publishing Limited 2014

Publisher: Susan Ross
Senior Editor: Danny Pearson
Publishing Assistant: Claire Morgan
Copyeditor: Cheryl Lanyon
Designer: Bigtop Design Ltd

2 4 6 8 10 9 7 5 3 1

CHAPTER 1

FORGOTTEN FRIENDS

Billy Button had green skin.

At the time, Liam didn't think anything of it. After all, Billy wasn't the same as other boys. He came and went as he pleased. One minute he wasn't there, the next he had appeared at Liam's side. Ready to play. Ready to cause trouble.

Billy could do anything he wanted. Nothing stopped him. Not rules. Not parents. Not teachers.

He could even walk through walls.

Because Billy wasn't real.

Liam hadn't thought about his imaginary friend for years. Until this morning, in fact. Until he had been rifling through the drawer beneath his bed and felt something cold and hard against his fingers.

He'd brought the object out and stared at it in amazement.

A big, green button.

He'd had it since he was five. His grandma used to let him play with the buttons from her sewing kit. He'd spend hours sorting them into different shapes and colours.

The big, green button was his favourite, and one day she said he could take it home.

It was the same day he met Billy.

Liam was playing in the garden on his own. No brothers or sisters. Not since the accident anyway. Not since they'd lost Marcus.

And Dad.

So he made up his own brother. A boy his own age, just a bit taller, with long arms and legs. Like a spider. A mop of unruly hair sat on Billy's head and his eyes shone like pinpricks of light.

At first, Billy would come whenever Liam held his grandma's button tight in his fist. Soon, he could call Billy without need of the button, although Liam always kept it in his pocket anyway. He was never lonely when Billy was around. Never scared. Billy always knew what to say to cheer him up, flashing that cheeky, lopsided grin.

Even Mum got used to Billy being around, although she couldn't see him, of course. Sometimes, she even set an extra place at dinner, not that Billy liked her cooking.

"Ugh, that's rank!" he'd complain, pulling the funniest faces. Liam would try not to laugh – and fail.

Mum didn't mind the giggling. She was just happy to hear Liam laugh again.

She wasn't so glad when Liam started blaming Billy for things.

"Billy ate the last custard cream, Mum. Not me."

"Billy lost my coat."

"Billy smashed your vase."

"Billy told me to run away…"

She lost her patience then. "You need to grow up," she snapped. "Forget about Billy. Live in the real world."

Eventually, Liam did exactly that. He went to school. Made new friends. Friends who were real. Who Mum could see.

And not one of them had green skin.

Billy simply faded away. Out of sight, out of mind. Until today. Until Liam found that button again.

He had it in his hand now, turning it over and over as he listened to Mr Newman call out the register. The plastic was cold, even though it was the hottest day of the year. It had always been the same and, until now, Liam had never thought it was odd.

Mr Newman continued through the names.

"Jon Mann?"

"Here."

"Helen Wright?"

"Here."

"Billy Button?"

Liam's head snapped up. "What?" he said out loud.

Mr Newman looked puzzled. "Liam? Is everything all right?"

Liam glanced around, feeling his face flush. Everyone was staring at him.

"Sorry, sir. It's just…" his voice trailed off. Someone sniggered at the back of the class. Liam swallowed, his mouth dry. "The last name on the register, sir. Wh-who was it?"

Mr Newman checked the computer screen. "Ben," he said. "Ben Clifton." He turned to peer at Liam. "Is that OK?"

Liam's cheeks were now burning hot. "Yeah, I'm… sorry, sir," he muttered. "Just thought you said something else."

Mr Newman shook his head and carried on with the register. Liam felt an elbow nudge him in the side.

"What was that about, you idiot?" said a fair-haired boy called Chris Hussey.

Liam shook his head, staring at his desk as if his life depended on it. He could still feel everyone's eyes on him. "Nothing," he grunted. "Just being stupid. It doesn't matter."

"Loser," Chris snorted, but he didn't mean it. Chris and Liam had been friends from the moment they'd met. Best friends.

The button in Liam's hand grew colder than ever.

CHAPTER 2

THE FACE IN THE DOORWAY

By lunchtime Liam was seriously freaking out. What was it with today? Yes, he'd been teased about his outburst during the register. He couldn't blame Chris. That's what you did – take the mickey out of your mates. Liam could cope with that.

It was the other stuff that bothered him. The stuff he couldn't explain.

The stuff about Billy.

He heard the name everywhere he went. Whispered as he barged his way down the corridor. Shouted across the playground. Snatches of conversations.

Billy Button.

Billy Button.

The same everywhere Liam went. That stupid, childish name over and over again.

Billy Button.

Billy Button.

It didn't make any sense. He'd never talked to anyone about Billy. Not even Chris. Not because he'd been embarrassed. It wasn't that. Billy just wasn't important any more.

Billy Button.

Billy Button.

Things got worse when he made his way to Geography, the last lesson before lunch. He was keeping his head down, just trying to get through the day without going insane. Then he walked past a kid from year seven.

"Did you hear what Billy Button did? I can't believe it."

Liam whirled around and grabbed the younger pupil by his jumper, ramming the kid into the lockers.

"What did you say?" Liam growled. "Who are you talking about?"

The boy's eyes were wide as he stammered his reply. "N-no one," he squeaked. "J-just someone we know."

"Billy Button?" asked Liam through gritted teeth.

The kid was shaking now. "I d-don't know who that is."

Liam wasn't having that. "Who put you up to this?" he snarled. "Who told you about Billy?"

The kid's mates had inched away from the lunatic from year nine. "I-I don't know what you're talking about," the boy squeaked. "P-please! Let me go."

Another voice cut in. Familiar and close at hand. "Liam!"

Chris pulled Liam away from the younger lad. "What are you doing?"

The year seven kid grabbed his bag and ran, scrabbling to get away from Liam.

Liam didn't know what to say. Chris slapped him on the shoulder.

"Seriously, mate. What's with you today?"

Liam shrugged. "It's nothing, honest."

"Didn't look like nothing to me. Since when have you picked on little kids?"

"I don't do that!" Liam insisted.

"You sure about that?" Chris said, pointing down the corridor. "That boy looked really scared."

Liam opened his mouth to reply, but stopped himself. What would he say? He was talking about my imaginary friend. Yeah, right. Chris would think he was bonkers.

Perhaps he was.

The bell rang.

"Come on," Chris said, gently shoving Liam towards the next class. "Let's get going before you really get into trouble."

Glowering, Liam thrust his hands in his pockets. His fingers brushed against the plastic button.

*

Chris didn't sit next to Liam in Geography. Instead he found a chair at the back of the class, next to Beverly Green. On any other day, Liam would have ribbed him about that.

Chris and Beverly sitting in a tree…

Chris would go bright red. Chris always went bright red when it came to girls – especially Bev.

K-I-S-S-I-N-G.

Not today. Liam didn't feel like mucking about. He didn't feel like doing anything. He tried to lose himself in his work, to forget about the year seven boy in the hallway. It was useless. Chris was right. The kid had been terrified. Because of him.

What was wrong with him? He never acted like that. He hated bullies. Always had.

It was Billy, Mum.

Liam's skin crawled as the thought crossed his mind. Now he was freaking himself out. He rubbed his eyes with the heels of his palms. His hands were clammy. Perhaps he was coming down with something. That would explain it. Loads of people had been off with a tummy bug.

It would explain why he was feeling so weird.

The bell rang. Lunchtime. Liam turned to Chris, but he was already gone.

It didn't matter. He'd see Chris in the dinner hall.

But he didn't. Chris was nowhere to be seen. Probably for the best. Liam didn't feel like talking to anyone anyway.

"Just get your lunch and get out of here," he thought to himself.

"Then what will we do?" a voice thought back.

"Shut up, Billy," Liam murmured as he slopped fruit salad into his bowl. He grabbed his tray from the serving hatch and looked for somewhere to sit.

A shoulder barged into him as he turned. Angular. Hard. Liam was knocked from his feet, his tray clattering against the floor. The bowl of fruit salad smashed against the tiles.

Liam jumped back up, looking for who'd knocked him over. There was no one there.

One of the dinner ladies bustled over to him. "You all right, love? Oh, look at all that fruit. Such a waste."

"I'm fine," Liam said, trying to ignore the feeling that everyone was staring at him for the second time that day. "Here, I'll clear that – "

He bent down to pick up the broken bowl and froze.

A face was looking at him through the dining hall's large double doors. A face that was there one second, gone the next. Nothing more than a blur – but Liam recognised it immediately. The black hair. The bright eyes.

The green skin.

CHAPTER 3

THE WRITING ON THE WHITEBOARD

They wanted to send Liam home after that. After he'd screamed out in the middle of the dining hall. There were a lot of questions. Was he feeling all right? Why had he shouted? Who was Billy?

Even Mr Newman had suddenly appeared by his side, as if by magic. "Do you need to sit down for a bit, Liam? You could go back to class, if you wanted? Where it's quieter."

Liam shook his head. "No, sir. I-I just feel a little…"

He didn't know what to say.

"Under the weather?" Mr Newman offered, trying to help. Liam nodded. "Well, see how you feel. Perhaps some fresh air will do you good."

Liam doubted it, but he did what he was told. He didn't want any more fuss. Usually he'd head straight for the playing fields to kick a ball about.

Not today. He found a tree and sat beneath the shadow of its branches, watching the other kids. Playing games on the basketball courts. Girls huddling beside the science block. Kids from year seven glancing nervously in his direction.

But they were all real. He was real. No green boys. No ghosts of the past.

And so it carried on for the rest of the day. Getting through the afternoon lessons, not really saying a word to anyone. Not even Chris. Not that his so-called mate came near. Chris was keeping his distance. Everyone was. Fine. He didn't need them anyway.

At three o'clock, Liam glanced at his watch. Nearly the end of school. About time. All he wanted to do was to get home, flop on the sofa and fire up the X-Box. Forget about everything else. Mum wouldn't mind. She'd still have work to do. She might even get pizza delivered for tea. Tomorrow would be different. Tomorrow would be better.

He didn't even realise he was tapping the green button against his desk.

Tap, tap, tap, tap.

At the front of the class, his English teacher, Miss Granger, was writing on the whiteboard. It was something about poetry, but Liam wasn't concentrating.

The teacher turned back to the class, but the words kept appearing behind her. It wasn't Miss Granger's neat handwriting. The letters were big and untidy – like a little kid's.

Scrawled across the board.

Remember me?

Liam heard someone whimper. He didn't even realise it was him. He was too busy watching more letters appear beneath the message.

Two simple letters.

B.B.

Billy Button.

That name. Following him everywhere. In the classrooms, in the playground, in the corridor. That face. Taunting him.

Billy Button.

Billy Button.

Liam's chest was tight. He couldn't breathe. He needed to get out, to get away from the whiteboard. To get away from Billy.

He stood up, his chair scraping against the floor.

"Liam?" Miss Granger asked, her eyes narrowing. "What is it? Are you OK?"

Liam laughed. Not like usual – this laugh was shrill, unfamiliar. The laugh of a crazy person. "Why's everyone asking me that today? Are you OK, Liam? What's wrong, Liam?"

Miss Granger started walking towards his desk, concern written all over her face.

"Everything's wrong," he yelled. "Everything!"

"Calm down," Miss Granger said, her voice strong, commanding. "There's no need to shout."

"No need?" Liam replied, pointing to the front of the class. "Look on the board, miss. Look at it! Look at the words!"

Miss Granger did as she was asked, shaking her head as she turned back to Liam. "You mean my notes? What about them?"

"No, not them," Liam said. "The message

underneath. From him. From Billy."

"From who?"

"Billy," Liam yelled. "Billy Button. There!"

Miss Granger's tone hardened. "There's nothing there, Liam."

"There is!" he insisted. He turned to Chris. "You can see it, can't you Chris?"

Chris shifted uncomfortably in his chair. "There's nothing there, mate."

It felt like Chris had just punched Liam in the face. "You're all in this together," Liam said quietly. He turned back to Miss Granger. "You. Mr Newman. All of you."

Miss Granger tried to reason with him, but he wasn't listening. The words on the board were changing in front of his eyes. Blurring. Liam blinked, trying to focus. Trying to read the message.

I REMEMBER YOU!

Liam screamed. A full-on, empty-your-lungs scream. Around him, his classmates tried to shuffle away from him on their chairs. Miss Granger shouted for him to calm down, telling one of the boys at the front of the class to get the head teacher. At the back of the room, someone sniggered.

A snigger he hadn't heard since the day he'd broken Mum's vase.

"It was Billy, Mum."

Not Liam. Always Billy. It was always Billy's fault.

Before he knew it, Liam was running. He bolted across the classroom, out into the corridor.

He couldn't hear anything else now. Not Miss Granger calling after him. Not his footsteps pounding against the floor. Just Billy's laughter, louder and louder.

He needed to get out, away from school. Away from everyone.

But he wasn't alone. Someone was running beside him, matching him step for step. Down the corridor. Out of the main doors. Towards the gates.

Someone Liam couldn't see, but knew was there.

CHAPTER 4

BYE-BYE, BILLY

Liam didn't stop running until he got home. He crashed through the front door, almost falling over the trainers Billy had left in the hall last night.

No. Not Billy. Liam. Liam had left them. Billy wasn't real.

Liam's mum was out of the kitchen in a heartbeat.

"I told you to put those away…" She took one look at his sweat-drenched face. "Baby, what's wrong?"

Liam hated her calling him baby. He wasn't a

baby. He was five years old…

No, not five, fifteen. He was fifteen. Of course he was.

Why couldn't he think straight? His skull felt like it was splitting in two.

Liam sat down hard on the bottom step of the stairs. "Don't feel good," he stammered, feeling his mum's cool hand on his brow.

"You're burning up."

He didn't feel hot. He felt cold. Freezing.

Mum cupped his face in her hands, checking his eyes as if she knew what she was doing. "Must be a virus. There's a lot of it going about," she said. She nodded to herself, pleased with her diagnosis. "Yeah, that's got to be it." She helped Liam back to his feet. "Get yourself up to bed. I'll make you some soup."

"I'm not hungry," Liam protested, but his mum wasn't having any of it.

"No arguments. You, bed, now!" she insisted and bustled back into the kitchen on a mission to find a can of chicken broth.

Liam hauled himself up the bannisters, his head throbbing. Past the step where he'd played with Billy. Across the landing where they knocked that photo of Dad off the wall. Into his bedroom, where he'd used to read Billy *The Beano* by torchlight when they were supposed to be asleep.

The window was open, cold air streaming into the room. Liam shivered as he pulled off his tie and shirt. He'd left his coat at school. His bag, too. Never mind. Chris would bring it round for him. Tomorrow. When everything was better.

He threw the shirt onto a chair and sat down on the bed, struggling out of his trousers. Something fell from his pocket, rolling across the carpet.

Something green.

The button.

Kicking off his trousers, Liam pushed himself from the bed and reached down for the button. His legs buckled beneath him and he fell onto his knees. He'd never felt so weak. He needed to sleep.

No! He needed to do something else first. He scooped up the button, hardly feeling it in his sweaty hand. Lurching back to his feet, he stumbled across to the window.

Drawing back his aching arm, Liam threw the button as far as he could. It arced across the garden, disappearing into the bushes beside the shed.

Liam let out a weak laugh.

Bye-bye Billy.

Downstairs, the phone started ringing. It was probably school. He didn't care. Liam staggered across the room and fell face-down onto his bed.

Tomorrow everything would be sorted. Billy would be gone and life would be back to normal. He just needed to sleep.

CHAPTER 5

LONG WALK HOME

The harsh barking of a dog woke Liam with a start. He sat bolt-upright and tumbled from his bed – landing in cold, wet mud.

What? He looked up from where he'd fallen. This couldn't be right? He wasn't at home, in his room, surrounded by his usual film and football posters. He hadn't even rolled from a bed.

Trembling, Liam put a hand out and pushed himself up from the ground. He wasn't shaking from the bitter wind that stung his face, or the chilly fog that hung heavily in the air. It was the shock of finding himself in the middle of a park.

How had he got here? He remembered getting home, talking to Mum – even flopping into bed. That's where he should be. Not here. Not sitting on a park bench, staring at a stream of joggers puffing and panting on the other side of the lake.

He hugged himself, trying to rub warmth into his cold limbs. His shirt was wet through.

His shirt? Why was he back in his school uniform? He'd taken that off, hadn't he? It should be crumpled on his bedroom floor as usual. He looked down at the shirt. Even beneath the mud splatters, it was grubby. Grey, where it had once been white. It looked like it hadn't been washed for weeks. His trousers were tattered too. And where were his shoes? He flexed his chilly toes, taking in the filthy, threadbare socks.

He looked around for his coat. His phone was in his pocket. He'd call Mum, find out where he was. Then he remembered. His coat was at school. He punched the park bench in frustration.

Rubber soles slapped against paving slabs. Liam looked up. A woman in a dark blue tracksuit was running towards him, blonde hair bobbing in a tight ponytail. She was looking straight ahead, listening to a pair of white, in-ear headphones.

"'Scuse me," Liam said, pushing himself up despite his stiff knees. Why did everything hurt? "Can you help me? I don't know where I am."

The runner didn't stop. She didn't even slow down.

Liam took a step forwards. "Please. I need help."

Perhaps she couldn't hear him over her music. Perhaps she didn't want to. The woman ran past, not even glancing in his direction.

As if he wasn't there.

"Thanks a bunch," he called after her. Shoving his hands into his pockets, Liam trudged towards a large, stone arch. That must lead out of the park. He needed to find a phone box. He'd phone home, reversing the charges. Mum wouldn't mind. This was an emergency.

He winced as he stood on a sharp stone. This was officially the worst morning ever.

*

Hobbling out of the park, Liam found a street he recognised. He was nearer to home than he'd thought. So far, so good.

He even found a phone box that hadn't been vandalised. Maybe luck was on his side after all.

He picked up the phone and dialled 100.

"Operator," said a bored female voice.

"Hello," Liam said eagerly. "I need to place a reverse charge call."

There was a pause on the other end of the line. "Hello?"

"I need to reverse the charges," he repeated, "call home…"

"Is there anyone there?"

Liam's knuckles went white around the phone. "Yeah. I'm here. Can you hear me? I need to call my – "

The line went dead. Liam let out a cry of anger and slammed the phone against the cradle.

"This. Can't. Be. Happening!"

His rage gave way to despair. He let the phone drop and it knocked against the back of the phone box, dangling from its cord. Liam screwed his eyes tight, willing himself not to cry. A tear splashed down onto the grimy floor before he wiped his eyes on the back of his hand. This wasn't helping. He'd just walk home. It shouldn't take him long, no more than half an hour. Forty minutes, tops. He might even be able to jump on a bus. If he explained to the driver what had happened, they might give him a free ride home. Mum could send the money to the bus company later.

But no buses would stop for him. It could have been the state of his clothes or the fact that he'd started coughing. Wet, hacking coughs that rattled in his chest. Probably the same reason no one on the street would look at him either, marching by as quickly as they could.

Eventually he made it home, limping as he walked up the front path. He searched his trouser pockets for his key, but instead pulled out a large, green button. The same button he had chucked from his bedroom window. Billy's button.

Liam tossed it aside as if it was red hot. It rolled across the drive and plopped down the drain. Good riddance!

"Mum," Liam yelled, banging on the door. "Mum, it's me."

There was no answer and no sign of her as he

peered through the kitchen window. She must have gone out. Typical!

He tried next door. Their neighbour, Mr Gibbs, was retired and only went out to collect his pension or get the morning paper. Liam pressed hard on the doorbell. When that didn't work he called through the letterbox. "Mr Gibbs. It's Liam. Are you there?"

Nothing.

It was the same at every house in the street. Surely they couldn't all be out? Trying not to cry, Liam sat on the low wall at the end of his street and stared at the pavement. Billy's green button was at his feet.

"Leave me alone," he screamed, standing up and booting the button away. "Leave me alone!"

The button skidded under a large, blue car.

Liam stood there, his chest heaving. He almost expected the button to get tossed back, but nothing happened. Of course it didn't. This was stupid. All of it.

A curtain twitched in the house behind him. Liam ran up the gate and hammered on the bright red front door. "Mrs Briggs! Mrs Briggs, can you hear me?"

If she could, she was doing a very good job of ignoring him. Billy let his head drop forwards, resting against Mrs Briggs's door. "Why is no one helping me?"

As if in answer, shouts drifted through the air. Not far away. Excited voices.

School!

He glanced at where his watch should have been. It must be break-time. Instead of snivelling outside his neighbours' houses, he'd go to school. Why hadn't he thought of that before? He'd find Mr Newman or Miss Granger. Then a smile spread across his face – Chris. Liam would see Chris.

He would know what to do. He'd be able to help. Of course he would. Chris was his friend.

CHAPTER 6

ALONE

The children were trooping back inside the school by the time Liam bolted through the gates. His feet were killing him now, huge holes ripped in his already ruined socks – but he didn't care. He looked around for Chris but couldn't see him. He wasn't in any of their usual spots. Never mind. He'd be inside by now.

Liam sprinted through the door, weaving in and out of pupils. He tried to remember what class they had after break. Was it French or History? It was hard to remember anything this morning.

Then he saw a familiar face. Miss Granger. He ran down the corridor, calling out her name.

"Miss Granger! Miss!"

She didn't stop.

"Miss, please!"

Catching up, he grabbed her arm. She let out a startled cry and span around.

"Who was that?" she snapped, glaring at the pupils behind Liam. "Who grabbed me?"

"It was me, miss," Liam blurted out, standing right in front of her. The other children shrugged and shook their heads.

"Kids!" Miss Granger muttered, rolling her eyes and turning back the way she'd been heading.

"Miss," Liam shouted, chasing after her. "It was me. Miss, can't you hear me?"

He ran past a door, the class inside catching his eye. His class. Giving up on Miss Granger, he grabbed the door handle. It wouldn't budge.

On the other side of the glass panel, his friends messed around as the lesson began. Mr Newman called for quiet. Slowly, the children settled, slouching in their seats.

There was Beverly, sitting at the back of the class with Chris. They were getting to be a right little couple.

Liam frowned. Chris was talking to the boy sitting beside him, a boy he didn't recognise. Not at first.

Then he realised who it was. The tall, lanky frame. The lopsided grin. The mop of dark hair.

Only one thing was different. This time his skin wasn't green.

"Billy," Liam hissed. His imaginary friend was sitting there, in his seat, joking with his best mate

– but looked real. Not a figment of anyone's imagination. Actual flesh and blood.

Liam tried the handle again. When it still wouldn't open, he rammed into the door with his shoulder. It flew open, slamming into the wall. Paper fluttered down from the noticeboards as everyone jumped, including Mr Newman. Good. Now they'd have to take notice of him.

"Whatever was that?" the teacher grumbled. He walked behind Liam and checked the door, pushing it shut again. "Must have been the wind…"

"Of course it wasn't," Liam shouted. "It was me. Me!"

But Mr Newman was walking away again, back to the front of the class, as if Liam hadn't said a thing.

"You can't see me, can you?" Liam realised. "None of you can."

He crossed to the first row of desks, slamming his hands on a table. He leaned into the face of the nearest pupil. Kevin Barnes. Class creep. Nervous as hell, usually.

He didn't even flinch.

"Kevin!" Liam yelled, right in the scrawny kid's face. "Can you hear me, Kevin? Kevin!"

Nothing. Liam cried out, trying to knock the boy's books from the table. Anything to cause a scene. Anything to be noticed.

His fingers swept through the books, like a ghost's.

Liam glared at his fingers as if they'd done it on purpose, and then tried again. He tried grabbing Kevin's pens, even his glasses. His hand slipped right through Kevin's smug face.

"I can't touch anything," Liam said out loud – not that it made any difference. "Why can't I touch anything?"

And all the time, Newman droned on at the front of the class.

"Shut up!" Liam screamed at the teacher. "Shut up! Shut up! Shut up!"

No reaction. Nothing at all. He turned to face Chris. "Chris, you can hear me, can't you? You know I'm here, right?"

He clambered around the desks to where Chris sat, tapping a pencil softly against the tabletop.

Tap, tap, tap, tap, tap, tap.

"Chris, this isn't funny. Don't do this. Please."

Tap, tap, tap, tap, tap, tap.

Liam couldn't breathe, his heart thudding against his chest. He turned on the black-haired boy sitting beside Chris. Billy. Looking so smug. So safe.

"You did this, didn't you?" Liam yelled, stabbing a finger at his not-so-imaginary friend. "I don't know how, but this is all your fault. It's always your fault."

Still Billy wouldn't look at him.

Liam bellowed in his smarmy face. "It was you!"

A ghost of a smile tugged at Billy's thin lips and he turned, looking Liam straight in the eye. "Of course I did, little Liam. It isn't nice being forgotten, is it?"

Liam staggered back. "You can see me," he gasped.

"What was that, Billy?" asked Mr Newman from the front of the class.

Billy turned his attention back to the teacher.

"Sorry sir, just thinking aloud."

Liam shook his head. "No. Don't ignore me. Not again. Don't you dare!"

The smirk continued to play across Billy's pale face. Sly. Triumphant.

"Don't. You. Dare." Liam launched himself at Billy. His hands went to grab Billy's school shirt, but passed straight through. Liam fell forward, moving too fast. He couldn't stop himself, couldn't stop himself passing through Billy's body and into the wall at the back of the class.

He tumbled through plaster and brick, landing in a heap outside the school, the mid-morning sun finally burning through the mist. He couldn't feel its heat. Couldn't feel anything at all.

Liam knelt on the ground and howled at the sky.

What had Billy done to him? What had he become?

The howl broke into uncontrollable sobs. He rocked back and forth, staring at his hands.

At his fingers.

They were green.

EPILOGUE

TWO YEARS LATER...

Chris Hussey picked up his bag. This was it. The final day of school. His last exam. Goodbye lessons. Goodbye homework. Goodbye boring old Newman.

Grinning, Chris threw the bag over his shoulder.

"Watch it," laughed Beverly, whacking him playfully in the arm. "You nearly hit me with that thing."

"Sorry." Chris smiled as his girlfriend bumped into a pile of textbooks. They thudded to the floor.

"Now look what you made me do," she moaned.

"Clumsy," he said, crouching to help.

Something caught his eye as he picked up the first book.

"What's wrong?" Beverly asked.

Chris showed her a name scribbled on the first page. "Look at this, Bev. Liam Chase."

Beverly shrugged. "So what?"

Chris scratched the back of his neck. "Didn't we use to have a Liam in our class?"

Beverly took the book from Chris's hands and slipped it back on the bookcase. "Not that I remember." She flashed him one of her brilliant smiles. "Come on, Face-ache, Billy will be waiting for us."

Chris grinned and followed her out of the classroom, pausing only as they passed the window.

"What now?" Beverly asked.

Chris shrugged. "Nothing," he said, but he was lying. There had been something, there in the window. A face he seemed to recognise – there one minute, gone the next. Glaring at him.

Chris shook his head. Just his eyes playing tricks on him. Besides, the face in the window had been green.

How stupid was that?

THE END